NORTHWEST C
INDIANS
COLORING BOOK

Illustrated by Tom Smith

Written by Tom and Diane Smith

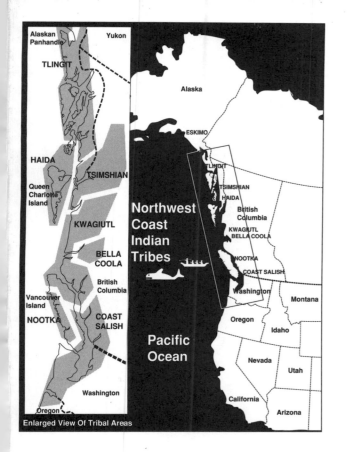

Enlarged View Of Tribal Areas

Copyright © 1993 Tom Smith. Published by Troubador Press, an imprint of Price Stern Sloan, Inc., a member of The Putnam & Grosset Group, New York, New York. Printed in the United States of America. Published simultaneously in Canada. All rights reserved. No part of this publication may be reproduced, stored in any retrieval system or transmitted, in any form or by any means, electronic, mechanical, photocopying, recording, or otherwise, without the prior written permission of the publisher.

12 11 10 9 8 7 6 5   ISBN: 0-8431-3879-3

Along the rugged west coast of North America, between Northern Oregon and the Alaskan Panhandle lies a strip of land cut off from the rest of the world by a series of high mountains that run along its eastern edge. The shores are rocky, dotted with inlets and thousands of small islands. It is the home of what are considered the tribes of the Northwest Coast Indians.

Isolated from the interior Plains Indians by vast mountains, these tribes developed a sophisticated culture and spiritualism that is unique to this area of the world. Their culture developed around the water, from which they got most of their food and they became skilled fishermen and sailors. As time passed, various families and groups spread out, thus establishing the variety of tribes that currently exists in the Pacific Northwest area. Some of the numerous tribes are indicated on the map.

Both animal and plant life were abundant here. Forests were thick and often impenetrable forcing the natives to settle on the shores where it was easier to build shelter. They lived in small beachfront villages scattered along the rocky coast in large "long houses" or "big houses," big enough for entire clans—40 to 60 people. As they built large cedar canoes for fishing and travel—as large as 30 to 60 feet long—they also learned about working the various woods that were provided by the abundant forests. As their carving skills increased, every aspect of their daily lives and culture became embellished with beautiful designs depicting their life and beliefs. Everything, from cookware to the massive totem poles, was intricately carved and painted.

This coloring book is in honor of the artistic peoples of the Northwest Coastal tribes. By providing you with examples of Northwest Coast styles and symbols, we hope to inspire in each of you an artistic vision of your own.

THE SPINDLE WHORL

The Spindle whorl was used for spinning the wool of the mountain goat into yarn, so that it could be woven into blankets and clothing. It was a round, flat disk, usually carved in wood about 4 to 8 inches across. A hole was drilled into the center where a wooden rod would go. When finished, it would look a little like a spinning top.

The Indians ventured high into the mountains to obtain the wool, making it very rare and used only for special garments. This is one of the reasons why spindle whorls were so highly prized and decorated.

Most of the wool went into the making of "Chilkat blankets." These were also known as dance capes and were considered the best example of a weaver's talents. They were used for ceremonial dances or as gifts for the most honored guest.

KILLER WHALE

The Killer Whale was the greatest hunter in the sea and was held in high esteem by the People. Killer whales hunted in packs like the wolf and were sometimes called sea wolves.

The People believed that the whales lived in villages at the bottom of the ocean. They believed that if a whale was injured in a hunt, it would capsize the hunting canoe and drag it down to the underwater Village of the Whales. The people in the canoe would then be transformed into whales themselves. Sometimes whales seen near shore were considered drowned relatives trying to communicate with their loved ones.

Since the People recognized that there were various species of whales, they grouped them in different clans, just like themselves. The Killer Whale was the most admired of all the whales and used as a powerful crest by many clans. It is one of the most often used designs, especially on totem poles and on the front of canoes.

BEAR

The Bear, also known as the "Elder Kinsman," was a subject of many legends. There are many stories, among most tribes, about women working in the woods who are abducted by bears. Instead of a beast, they find such a kind and generous soul that they marry him and have bear children. Since bears were often seen in the mouth of rivers and sometimes in the ocean itself, there are also stories of a great Sea Bear, which is part bear and part whale.

The People admired the bear for his human qualities and great hunting and fishing abilities. When a bear was killed, it was often taken to the house of the chief where it was sprinkled with eagle down—a symbol of respect and greeting—and welcomed as a honored guest.

Many families used the bear as their clan crest. He is probably the figure seen most often on totem poles as well as boxes, bowls and other carved items. His smiling face is on most gift items as a symbol of welcome and friendship.

HOUSE POST

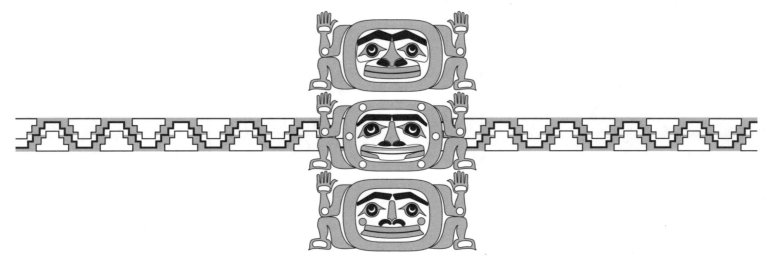

The Four House Posts would hold up the roof of the long house. The long houses were very large, sometimes 40 to 60 feet long. They were made out of long planks of cedar which were split with stone tools.

A number of families, considered a clan, would live in cubicles built into the sides of the long house. This way the children, parents and grandparents would all have their own cubicles, but still be under the same roof. Usually there was a long, wide trench dug into the center of the long house where each family would have their cooking fires. This is where they would gather for family meals and clan meetings.

The four house posts would be the first to go up when building a long house. The posts were often very thick, as they had to hold up a great deal of weight. Special artists were hired to carve and paint the house posts and the clan crests for the totem pole that went in front of the long house. When completed, the totem pole would identify the clan and all the families living in the long house.

BEAVER

The Beaver showed the People how to cut down trees and build houses so they could be safe and warm in the long, wet winters. The Beaver was considered an old and wise creature. Legends tell of how the first beaver came to be:

A woman with long, thick brown hair dammed a small stream one hot summer to make a pond in which she could swim. Her husband wanted her to go back to work, but she was much too hot to obey. She swam in the pond for so long that it became a lake. Her leather apron flapped in the water and slowly turned into a tail; her long brown hair grew all over her body. And so, as she swam about, she became the first beaver.

The Beaver can be seen carved on many things. She is usually seen with her large, flat tail drawn up against her stomach or her tail protruding from her mouth, especially on totem poles, where space is limited.

RAVEN

The Raven, also known as the "Trickster," is a favorite character of the People. He was one of the most important creatures in their folklore. He put the sun and moon into the sky, the rivers and trees onto the land and brought the People out of the clam shell so they could live on the Earth.

Raven was embodied with supernatural and magical powers. He could fly to the stars or swim under the sea, and make anything happen just by wishing it. He was playfully mischievous and usually motivated by greed, which drove him to trick, cheat and tease. However, in most of his tricks, poor Raven was usually the loser.

Raven was such a powerful character in the mythology of all the tribes, that his image was used as a family crest only by the most powerful families. The only crests of living animals that had more power than the Raven were the Eagle and Thunderbird crests, which were used mainly by the families of chiefs. Raven can be seen carved on many of the items that the People used, from the totem poles down to the spoons that they ate with.

SALMON

The Salmon was a vital food source of the People. They were great fishermen, catching fish in rivers as well as out in the ocean. They built huge fishing canoes out of cedar trees which were sometimes big enough to hold up to 35 fishermen.

Salmon had many uses for the People, who were never wasteful. They smoked and dried it over fires to preserve it for the long, cold winter. It was also a food they could easily pack and eat on long journeys. Salmon oil was an excellent cooking oil as well as a spice for other foods. The oil was also used to light lamps and as a healing salve in herbal medicines.

Since there are five different species of salmon, the People believed them to be of different clans living in separate villages in the sea, just like the whales.

PORTRAIT MASK

Portrait Masks were hand carved and worn during battles, spiritual rites, dance ceremonies and sometimes just for decoration. The young girl mask above is a portrait mask. They were sometimes carved from living people to represent a certain characteristic of that person.

During the warm summer months the People wore very little clothing so almost all of the tribes painted and tattooed their faces and bodies to enhance their natural beauty. Bear grease was used to ensure the adherence of paints used for body and face decorations. The grease, being shiny, also prevented sun and wind burn. When the white man first encountered the People, they considered them unclean because of the thick grease and paint they always wore. This was untrue as the Indians bathed daily and changed the painted designs 2 or 3 times a day.

Portrait masks were often used in elaborate dance ceremonies. At the beginning of a dance, a dancer might wear a portrait mask to represent a certain person. As the dance progressed the mask would be changed to that of another creature or spirit to show the transformation that the dancer would go through as a story was played out.

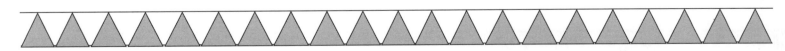

SHAMAN'S MASK

A Shaman's Mask was used to portray a Shaman in ritual dances and ceremonies. The Shaman was a spiritual guide and healer and was sometimes referred to as a medicine man by the white man. Usually the oldest and wisest person of the clan, the Shaman had a great wealth of information about herbal medicines, beliefs, rituals and the spiritual knowledge of the People.

They told stories and tales of days gone by so no one would forget the clan history. They helped people in times of trouble, giving advice on private matters or matters which affected the whole tribe. They counseled the chiefs and tended to the sick with herbal remedies and ritual dances, which helped dispel bad spirits. The Shaman was a doctor, priest and counselor all rolled into one. Many of the northern tribes had women as herbal healers and Shamans.

COPPER

The Copper was used as a form of money and wealth among the People. They were made out of "Native" copper, which was found in the land where they lived. This copper was very hard to obtain and considered very rare. The raw copper was traded from the Athabaskan Indians from the Interior Plains or in later times from the white man.

Coppers were beaten into the shape above and usually painted or engraved with traditional designs. Most Coppers were fairly large, often 2 to 3 feet tall and a foot across.

One of the most interesting aspects of the Copper is that they were given names so that their worth and heritage could be passed on. A Copper was only worth what it was last traded for and it could only be traded for a larger amount the next time around. Consequently, some Copper values became incredible, worth the total of 1500-2000 blankets, a couple of war canoes and hundreds of boxes and bowls. No matter what the original value was, the next person who wanted it had to trade more in exchange for it. Only the richest and most powerful could afford the price of an old Copper.

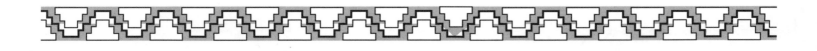

WOLF

The Wolf was considered the greatest of all hunters. His spirit was the power which all hunters tried to instill in themselves. It was his keen sense of smell, his sharp eyesight, his powerful legs and his knowledge and cunning that a good hunter called upon to succeed.

The People felt a deep kinship to wolves since these creatures also lived and hunted in family groups. The best hunters took the Wolf as their spiritual guide and used his image on their personal possessions.

One legend has it that a great white wolf with supernatural powers transformed himself into a killer whale so that he could hunt in the sea. It is believed that this is the reason why killer whales have white markings and hunt in packs in the water as wolves do on land. Because of this great hunting skill, the Wolf can be seen carved and painted on the front of many canoes as well as totem poles and hunting tools.

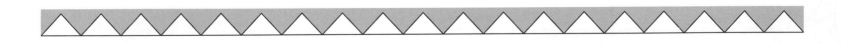

STORAGE BOX

The Storage Box, also known as the "Bentwood Box," was a special box used to store all the blankets and prize possessions of a family. The sides of the box were made from a single piece of cedar wood which was cut with four deep grooves on the back. The board was then steamed until the wood became soft. It would then be bent into a four-sided box shape. The ends were tied together with cedar twine and the bottom piece added to hold the sides in shape while the wood dried. The top was made from a thick slab of wood which was carved out to fit over the top of the box.

All sides of the box were painted brightly and the family crests were carved into the front and back. Rows of cowrie shells were inlaid into the top. Special artists were hired to make the boxes and they were handed down from generation to generation or given away as gifts to the most honored guests.

The same "bentwood" technique was used to make much smaller, lidless boxes that were not painted. These smaller boxes were actually called bowls and used to eat out of, since they were so tightly constructed, they could actually hold water.

OWL

The Owl's nocturnal habits were often associated with the mysterious and the occult by most of the People. Owl was often thought to be the main spirit helper of the Shaman and was considered to be a messenger of bad fortune and death. Great spiritual meaning was attached to any contact with owls in the forests. Among the northern tribes it was believed that when a owl flew over a person's head, they were certain to meet with doom.

Because of his strong underworld spiritual reputation, Owl usually appeared only on the tools and necessities of the Shaman. Owl was also sometimes depicted on the burial or mortuary totem pole, marking graves.

FROGS

The Frog is considered a good, friendly creature and is most often seen wearing a wide grin. Legend has it that until recently, no frogs lived on the Queen Charlotte Islands, home of the Hiada Indians. A Hiada story tells of a Frog Chief who ran into a black bear while traveling along the Island. The black bear was amused by the hopping Frog Chief and tried to step on it, just for fun. The little frog escaped by hopping between the bear's legs. The Frog Chief ran back to his village telling all the other frogs of his terrifying experience. Fearing this huge creature would find their village, the frogs packed their belongings and left the island for good, hoping they'd never meet another bear.

Frog images were carved on almost everything the People used especially house posts, bowls and totem poles where he is usually seen peeking out from under another creature. Many tribal Shamans considered him a helpful spirit to call upon. The Hiada carved frogs on all their house posts, believing that this would keep the poles from falling over.

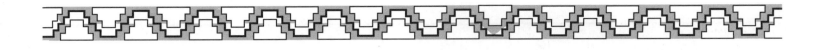

THUNDERBIRD

The Thunderbird was considered the most powerful of all the spirits. When he blinked his eyes, lightning flashed. When he opened his wings, thunder roared. He ate whales and carried two Lightning Snakes under his wings which he used to spear whales with. He lived high in the mountaintops among the clouds.

Thunderbird was considered by all of the tribes to be the highest of all the chiefs. Only the most powerful chief in the tribe was allowed to use the crest of the Thunderbird.

Thunderbird is almost always seen at the top of a totem pole with his powerful wings spread out. He is quite often painted on the front of long houses with a whale clutched in his powerful claws. You can always tell Thunderbird by the curved appendages on his head. These appendages were considered by most to be symbols of his power.

Thunderbird is one of the few mythological creatures used by almost all American Indian societies across the nation.

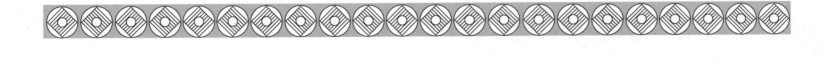

IMAGINATIVE
COLOR & STORY ALBUMS
FROM TROUBADOR PRESS

All About Horses	The Great Whales
Ballet	Horse Lovers
Cats & Kittens	Hot Rod
Cowboys	Mother Goose
Dogs & Puppies	North American Indians
Dolls	North American Sealife
The Enchanted Forest	Northwest Coast Indians
The Enchanted Kingdom	Tropical Fish
Exotic Animals	Unicorn
Giants & Goblins	Wonderful World of Horses

Also look for our Troubador Funbooks, ColorPops, *and*
punch-out and assemble Action *and* Play Sets.

Troubador Press books are available wherever books are sold or can be ordered directly from the publisher.
Customer Service Department, 390 Murray Hill Parkway, East Rutherford, NJ 07073

TROUBADOR PRESS
an imprint of
PRICE STERN SLOAN